Happy Birthday, SpongeBob!

by J-P Chanda

illustrated by Heather Martinez

SCHOLASTIC INC.

New York Toronto London Auckland Sydney
Mexico City New Delhi Hong Kong Buenos Aires

Stephen Hillenburg

Based on the TV series *SpongeBob SquarePants*® created by Stephen Hillenburg
as seen on Nickelodeon®

ISBN 0-439-76095-X

12 11 10 9 8 7 6 5 4 3 2 1   5 6 7 8 9 10/0

Printed in the U.S.A.   23

First Scholastic printing, September 2005

It was  birthday!
SPONGEBOB'S

"I hope there will be  and !" said .

GIFTS   CAKE   SPONGEBOB

"I love  and

BALLOONS   PARTY HATS

and !"

KRABBY PATTIES

"Do **you** know what day it is?" asked .

SPONGEBOB

GARY

"Meow?" 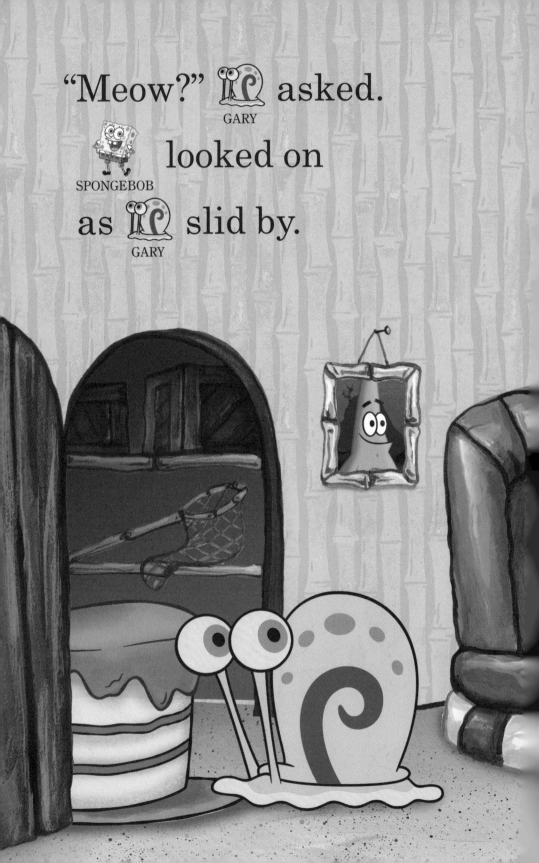 GARY asked.

SPONGEBOB looked on

as GARY slid by.

Did  forget
my birthday?
wondered .

was pushing

a big BOX.

"Is that a GIFT?"

asked SPONGEBOB.

"No, it is my new ,"

CHAIR

said .

SANDY

 sat on the .

SANDY   BOX

 did not say

SANDY

"Happy Birthday."

"Do **you** know

what day it is?"

 asked his friend

SPONGEBOB

 . "It starts with

PATRICK

a B...."

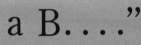

"I know! I know!"

said .
PATRICK

" ⚪ Day! 🏀 Day!
BUBBLE   BASKETBALL

🐝 Day?"
BUMBLEBEE

🧽 shook his head.
SPONGEBOB

Did everyone forget

the  and ?

GIFTS   CAKE

Did everyone forget

the  and
BALLOONS   PARTY HATS

and   ?
KRABBY PATTIES

wondered   .
SPONGEBOB

went to work.

The was empty!

"Hello?" called out.

SPONGEBOB

walked in

SQUIDWARD

and stood next to a .

TABLE

"What are you holding?"

asked SPONGEBOB .

"This is my new wig," said  .

SQUIDWARD

 put the  on his

SQUIDWARD   MOP

head.

" 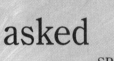 , do you know

what day it is?"

asked .

"It is a day to make !" said MONEY MR. KRABS.

"Into the kitchen, SPONGEBOB!"

"It looks like everyone forgot my birthday," said  .

SPONGEBOB

"No 🎁 , no 🎂 , and

GIFTS   CAKE

no 🎈 for me."

BALLOONS

"  !" called.

SPONGEBOB   MR. KRABS

"Come in here!"

"Surprise!" everyone yelled.

"Happy Birthday,  !"

SPONGEBOB

It was a big party

with  and !

GIFTS   BALLOONS

There were ...

PARTY HATS

Happy Birthday, SpongeBob!

. . . and  **KRABBY PATTIES**

with **CANDLES** on top!

"You did not forget!"

said **SPONGEBOB** . "Hooray!"